hoe

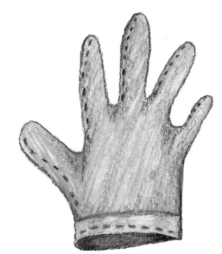

work
glove

trowel

The Rosy Fat Magenta Radish

by Janet Wolf

Little, Brown and Company

Boston Toronto London

Jim

Nora's Mom

Willy

First Edition

Library of Congress Cataloging-in-Publication Data
Wolf, Janet, 1957–
    The rosy fat magenta radish / by Janet Wolf.
        p.   cm.
    Summary: Relates the excitement and rewards of a child's first gardening experience.
    ISBN 0-316-95045-9 :
    [1. Gardening—Fiction.   2. Radishes—Fiction.]
I. Title.
PZ7.W81914Ro   1990
[E]—dc19   89-15463
                                                                CIP
                                                                AC

10 9 8 7 6 5 4 3 2 1

WOR

Joy Street Books are published by
Little, Brown and Company (Inc.)

Published simultaneously in Canada
by Little, Brown & Company (Canada) Limited

Printed in the United States of America

This book is for some gardeners in my family :

Ruth Neubauer,
Trude Spear and
Fred Wolf.

Nora

All week long, Nora has been waiting for Saturday.

"Slow down and chew your food," says Mom.

Nora tries to chew each bite, but her neighbor Jim is already outside and she does not want him to start without her. He pulls the red cart across the street and through the garden gate.

Jim and Nora have spent all week getting ready. Finally, Saturday has come. Today they will plant the garden.

Nora and Willy race out the back door.

"Hello, Nora." Jim smiles. "Hello, little monster," he says to Willy.

"We're ready!" says Nora.

First, they go to the tool shed. It is dark and smells like mushrooms. Nora likes to pretend elves live there.

Jim finds all the right tools and they load up their arms.

Outside, Nora studies the seeds and plants. The seeds come in bright, colorful packages. The tiny plants have long names on little plastic signs. The rhubarb and tomato plants are big: Jim bought them early and babied them in his warm kitchen window.

Jim picks up a flat of tomatoes. "These are ready to find a home of their own," he says. "Where do you think they should go?"

Nora finds the sunniest place in the garden. "Here!" she cries.

Jim carries the box over. Nora can hardly wait to start planting.

"Here, fill this." Jim hands Nora the watering can. She needs two hands to carry back the heavy full can.

"Do I get to plant now?" Nora asks.

"First help me with these," replies Jim. He crouches down and digs with a trowel. Then he gently nudges out a tomato plant. Its dirt and roots are shaped like a box. Carefully, he lowers it into the hole, pours in water, and pats the soil smooth. Then he scratches in fertilizer and adds more water.

"Okay," says Jim, "your turn!" He reaches deep down in his back pocket, pulls out a packet of seeds, and hands it to Nora.

On the front of the packet is a picture of a radish the color of Nora's favorite paint at school: magenta. A rosy fat magenta radish!

Jim and Nora take the package to a small patch near the kitchen window.

"Draw a line with your finger," he says. "Not too deep. Just up to your thumbnail."

Nora rips open the package. She pushes her thumb lightly in the soil and draws a line. Then she plants the seeds in a row. She pats the soil smooth and waters the flat dirt.

"When will there be radishes?" she asks.

"Water every day," says Jim, "and soon you'll see."

Later that afternoon Nora pretends she is in a kingdom far, far away. She is a famous royal gardener.

"You can be my assistant, Willy," she says. "We are growing royal radishes fit for a king!"

Early the next morning, Nora runs out to her radish patch. She looks for some magenta peeking out of the soil.

"No radishes yet, Willy. Tomorrow for sure."

Each morning, Nora runs out to look. Each morning she sees dirt with a sign.

Meanwhile, Jim's tomato plants begin creeping up the poles, his lettuce becomes round, his rhubarb grows large leaves, and his strawberries are almost ready for picking.

Jim picks weeds and waters his vegetables. Nora picks weeds and waters her dirt patch.

"Do you think we picked the radishes out by mistake, Willy?" she asks.

Then one morning some small green leaves peek out of the soil.

But they don't really look like the long leaves in the picture on the packet. And they grow in a mishmash. Jim's vegetables grow in straight rows.

"Keep watering," he says. "They'll get bigger."

The next day, Jim and Nora pick out a round ripe lettuce for her mother's salad. And they pull some pink rhubarb stalks and pick red strawberries for her mother's pie.

"How scrumptious!" Her mother loves them. "Let's invite Jim for our big family dinner on Sunday. I'll cook something special, and we'll have a great big salad topped with lots of your radishes!"

Nora is very quiet. Sunday is only five days away.

"They will be ready by then, won't they?" Mom asks Nora.

"Oh, yes," says Nora. "They will."

Sunday dinner:
lamb
potatoes
string beans
bread
strawberry/rhubarb pie
salad stuff
Nora's radishes!

Wednesday, Thursday, and Friday go by. The little leaves slowly get bigger. They start to look more like the leaves on the radish packet.

"But no magenta part," Nora says to Willy on Saturday. "It will come up by tomorrow, though."

On Sunday afternoon, Nora helps her mom spread out the beautiful linen tablecloth Jim brought them from Ireland. They pick roses and put them in the vase Nora made at school.

"Quick, Nora," says Mom, "I see Jim coming through the garden gate. Go pick your radishes for the salad!"

Nora walks slowly out to her radish patch.

She stares at the long green leaves. Then she stares at the radish sign with its long green leaves and rosy magenta part underneath. Then slowly she bends down to get a closer look. . . .

All of a sudden Nora grabs a fistful of leaves and yanks as hard as she can.

Out pops a whole bunch of radishes! Rosy fat magenta radishes!

"Look, Mom!" she cries, running into the kitchen. "Radishes for dinner!"

When dinner is over, and everyone's stomachs are stuffed, just one rosy fat magenta radish is left at the bottom of the bowl . . . but not for long!

The crispy magenta part crunches tartly in Nora's mouth. Tomorrow she'll pick more. Next year she'll plant twice as many!

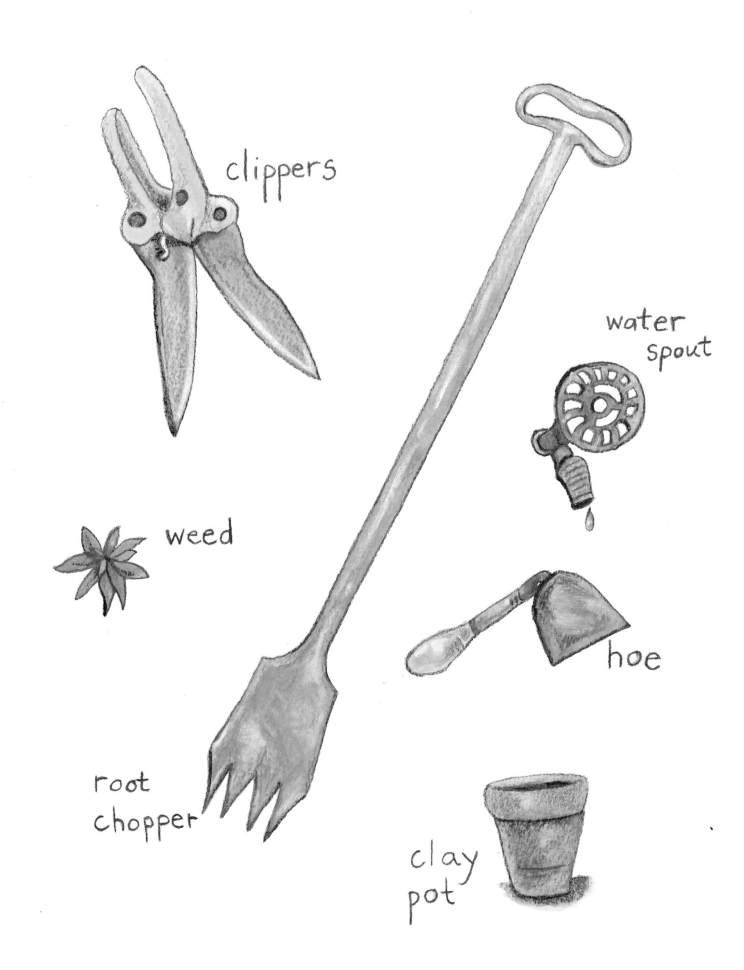

clippers

water spout

weed

hoe

root chopper

clay pot